THE MAGIC RING

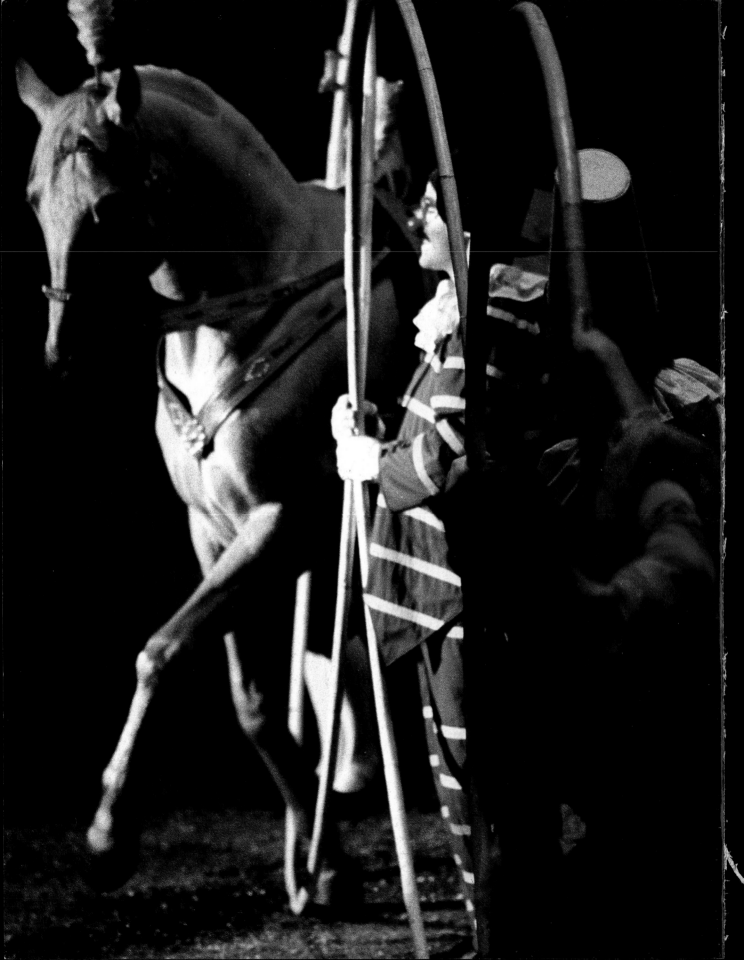

THE MAGIC RING

A YEAR WITH THE BIG APPLE CIRCUS

HANA MACHOTKA

INTRODUCTION BY
PAUL BINDER
ARTISTIC DIRECTOR
AND FOUNDER OF
THE BIG APPLE CIRCUS

WILLIAM MORROW & COMPANY, INC. ★ NEW YORK

To Otakar, Jarmila, Lida, and Milu

There are many people I would like to thank for making this book possible: Ron Smith and Ron Monroe for introducing me to the magic of the Big Apple Circus; Abe Menasche, who encouraged my vision and saw it through with endless artistic and technical advice; Paul Binder, for his faith in my work and his enormous contribution to this project; Dominique Jando for his vast store of information; and most of all, the performers themselves, who welcomed me into their lives and homes and cheerfully tolerated my long presence and endless questions. My special thanks go to Cheryl Jones, Carol Mark, and Howard Wahlberg of the circus staff, and to David LeBlanc, Michael O'Mahoney, and Michael LeClair of the tent crew.

Thanks also to Nikon Professional Services for the loan of equipment; Abe Sloan, Katherine Plumb, Kay Haran, and my mother for editorial help; my editor, Andrea Curley, for getting me through my first book; and the art director, Ellen Friedman, for her exquisite design. Thanks especially to my husband, Ed Marritz, for his constant advice and support, and to my children, Ilya and Leda, for putting up with my absences.

Text and photographs copyright © 1988 by Hana Machotka
Introduction copyright © 1988 by The New York School for Circus Arts, Inc.
All rights reserved.
No part of this book may be reproduced or utilized in any form or by any means,
electronic or mechanical, including photocopying, recording or by any information storage and retrieval system,
without permission in writing from the Publisher.
Inquiries should be addressed to
William Morrow and Company, Inc.
105 Madison Avenue
New York, NY 10016.
Printed in Singapore.
1   2   3   4   5   6   7   8   9   10
Library of Congress Cataloging-in-Publication Data
Machotka, Hana.
The magic ring.
Summary: Briefly surveys the history of circuses
and describes the growth, rehearsals, performances,
and personnel of the successful one-ring circus
known as the Big Apple Circus.
1. Big Apple Circus—Juvenile literature.
[1. Big Apple Circus.   2. Circus]   I. Title.
GV1821.B48M33   1988   791.3   87-28230
ISBN 0-688-07449-9
ISBN 0-688-08222-X pbk.

Hana Machotka just appeared one day, or so it seemed to the performers pictured in this book. Most of them hardly noticed. Yet she was around for almost a full year. Hana (who is not pictured in this book) is very quiet, very unprepossessing. But her work, as you can see on the following pages, speaks eloquently for her.

So, it seems, does the work of most circus artists. You might not notice Marie Pierre Benac or Phil Beder or Ricardo Gaona or Bill Woodcock if they were to sit next to you at a lunch counter. But in the ring these very ordinary people are capable of the most extraordinary things. Their discipline and technique, honed by years of practice and performance, propel them through moments alive and pulsing with excitement, wonder, and awe: Marie Pierre doing a double somersault on the Russian Barre; Phil twisting a full pirouette somersault through the air; Richie doing a slow double layout from the flying trapeze; or Bill calmly, almost invisibly, coaxing Toto the elephant to walk on his hind legs.

Hana started her "year with the Big Apple Circus" with the idea of doing a children's book about Katja Schumann, our world-renowned equestrienne. What could be more appealing to kids—lovely horses and their lady trainer? But Hana was confronted with something else—Katja's hours of painstaking exercise and practice, her longer hours of study and patience with her animals—developing her technique and their athletic conditioning, developing their technique and her presentation. Hours and days and weeks and months.

Watching Katja and others, it quickly became evident to Hana that Circus is adult stuff, the stuff of dreams—or of potential nightmares. Bodies flying through the air; humans facing wild beasts; taming creatures of flight; confrontations between masked figures; falls and stumbles; bright, flashing colors; loud sounds . . . It became evident that Circus, when done right, is a dream come true, a nightmare turned right.

We've all had "falling" dreams. Imagine being able to turn them into "flying dreams." There is a tribe in Malaysia that teaches its children how to do just that. The child's first success at a "flying dream" is the beginning of a rite of passage into adulthood. But isn't dealing with fear and the unknown the prime reason for all tribal rituals? Will we starve? Will it freeze before the harvest? Will a new chief be born? Will the winter end? What happens when I die? Will everything chaotic and confusing be understood enough for us to survive?

Circus is the modern genre of theater that comes closest to the original tribal ritual form. Processionals, music, confrontations, masked clowns, beasts, sensuality—controlled chaos turned into natural beauty. No wonder children adore it. It cuts directly to primal emotions. No need for interpretation. Real people actually flying, confronting, balancing, falling, making order out of chaos and—underline this—doing it with grace and beauty. And adults? The ritual, when artists create it, strips away their defenses and pretenses, touching them in a way that no other theatrical form does—in their heart and lungs and belly and nervous system. They laugh and shout and applaud with delight.

Are these then "ordinary people" presenting this show? The answer, of course, is yes; but they are artists as well. Look closely, as Hana's camera does, and you will see that what emerges is a picture of inner intensity and determination of a type rarely seen anywhere.

At the Big Apple Circus we measure performers by two very strict standards: their technical excellence and their ability to communicate emotional involvement in their presentation, their "contact" with the audience. The result is a series of virtuoso moments (don't call them "tricks") presented just for you, their public.

Balance, Jimmy Tinsman and David Dimitri remind us, is a system of movement, not stasis. And if you don't get the complete message from them (sometimes their movement is so refined, you hardly notice!) Michael Christensen (Mr. Stubs) and Jeff Gordon (Gordoon) will resort to the other extreme and fall, and laugh you will.

But wait . . . "still" photography is also a "system of movement," is it not? Such is the effect of Hana's photography—carefully chosen moments, carefully composed by the quiet eye behind the lens—presented just for the satisfaction of the public, you. Her book is a celebration of joy. It captures the essence of the performers, their animal partners, and the special environment in which they work.

Hana listens to her audience. And I know you will show your appreciation in much the same way as you have over the years for her subject, the Big Apple Circus.

ARTISTIC DIRECTOR AND FOUNDER
THE BIG APPLE CIRCUS

★

C O N T E N T S

INVITATION TO A CIRCUS

As the band strikes up a rousing melody, you step inside the blue-and-white tent with the big red stars. Your body starts to relax, your eyes widen in anticipation, and your pulse quickens to the music. Looking around, you notice the sawdust ring at the center: it's small and close enough to touch. It stands empty for now, but the cries of the popcorn vendors, the children squirming in their seats, and the exuberant music all tell you that the show is about to begin.

★ 1 ★

As you snuggle into your seat and dip your hand into the popcorn box, the lights go down, the music mellows, and a cool blue mist rolls into the ring. Out of the darkness emerge two enchanting horses. They frolic around the ring, kicking up their hooves, their shiny coats and flowing manes sparkling in the blue light. When their playful dance ends, they vanish into the shadows as magically as they had appeared.

Suddenly the lights come up as acrobats tumble into the ring, jumping, somersaulting, and juggling hoops. Colorful costumes glitter under the spotlights like a changing kaleidoscope as the acrobats scramble over one another to form a human pyramid. It quickly disperses as tall men in long, striped pants and carrying umbrellas stride into view. They are followed by equally tall ladies in big beautiful hats. An elephant appears, stands on his hind legs, and walks across the sawdust ring. The children scream with delight.

The one-ring circus is inviting, intense, and immediate! Sit next to the ring and feel the dirt fly in your face from galloping hooves. Giggle at the outrageous antics of the clowns. Look right into the performers' eyes, and see the sweat on their foreheads as muscles strain to perform incredible feats. Find yourself wanting to fly through the air with them, dance on a wire, and gambol with exotic animals. If you've caught circus fever, you aren't alone. At the Big Apple Circus, America is rediscovering the magic of the one-ring circus!

A LONG HISTORY

Human beings have been celebrating life through various forms of the circus since history has been recorded. Acrobatics developed in China about four thousand years ago. There is evidence in Egyptian wall paintings that acrobats, musicians, and dancers entertained villagers. The Egyptians, Greeks, and Romans, fascinated by the training of wild animals, kept game preserves and zoos. In the third century B.C. a menagerie parade in Egypt lasted from sunrise to sunset and included deer, rhinoceroses, elephants, ostriches, buffaloes, asses, bulls, horses, and lions. The Greeks trained lions to pull chariots, bears to do tricks, and horses to dance. In the Greek hippodrome (an oval racing stadium), horsemanship developed as a spectator sport. At the Circus Maximus (a Roman stadium used for races and games), an elephant is said to have walked on a tightrope. An early form of clown appears in ancient Greek and Roman plays.

The tradition of roving entertainers continued through the Middle Ages and Renaissance in fairs, plays, and marketplace performances. But it was not until about 1770 that many of these early circus elements came together in England in a dramatic way. Philip Astley, a spectacular horseman, enclosed his trick riding show in a ring within an outdoor amphitheater. The show was such a success that he added a roof, lights, music, acrobats, and comics. And so the circus as we know it was born. It flourished in England and spread quickly to the rest of Europe and to America.

In America in 1793 the first circus was founded by John Bill Ricketts in Philadelphia. Later, he established a permanent building in New York City. New York would become home to fifteen permanent circus buildings at various times over the next hundred years.

Many of the early circuses were mobile, performing under tents or in the open air. Sideshows and menageries, originally developed as separate enterprises, were later added as attractions. In the early days, the circus was considered adult entertainment to which children were often brought.

Because people were fascinated by natural curiosities, the circus proved immensely successful.

With bad roads and no streetlights, travel was hazardous for the early circuses. When a uniform rail gauge and a device for loading the wagons onto the cars were invented, circuses could travel much farther by rail, spurring on their rapid growth. As circus empires grew, so did personal fortunes. The trip from the railroad station into town became an elaborate circus parade, complete with beautifully carved wagons drawn by up to forty horses. Bringing up the rear was the calliope, tooting out its lilting melodies.

When P. T. Barnum's circus merged with that of James Bailey, the three-ring circus was born. When this combined once more with the great Ringling Brothers Circus, the result was truly "The Greatest Show on Earth." Circus had reached the height of commercialism, big business, and razzle-dazzle spectacle.

By the turn of the century, there were hundreds of circuses crisscrossing the United States. Circus promoters now directed their marketing at children, thus helping to create the idea that the circus was children's entertainment.

With the Great Depression, many circuses failed. Later, with the coming of television, fewer people ventured out to see live performances, and the few remaining circuses struggled to maintain a meager existence. With only a few dozen circuses left in America, "The Greatest Show on Earth" dominated the circus world. Until, one day, something unexpected happened. . . .

T he Big Apple Circus at Battery Park City may have turned me into a circus freak," began a review in a New York newspaper, *The Villager.* "The sandy clearing, decked with motley flags of silk, was briskly windblown and the billowing tent seemed ready to take to the sky. . . . Its incredible exuberance perceptively dwarfed the World Trade Center. . . . One ring is more than three, it appeared. Here man is the measure of all things." Thus Anne Melfi described the modest beginning of an exciting new arrival.

On WNYC radio, Leah Frank described the new sensation this way: "Perhaps because of the intimacy of the small tent, the acrobats create the most thrilling American circus I've ever seen. . . . It's so obvious that the performers are reaching into their core to give out 125 percent of themselves, they manage to generate a field of energy and love that's immediately contagious . . . it brings back childhood memories for those who remember the big touring circus tents, and it's evocative of another, simpler day when performers and audience, both adults and children, loved one another with unabashed pleasure. . . . At the end of the performance I saw, the entire audience was on its feet cheering, applauding, and yelling their approval of this totally pleasing show."

With reviews like these, and attendance far exceeding all expectations, Paul Binder knew he had created something special when on July 20, 1977, his one-ring circus opened. He had taken a chance on a dream, and that dream was taking off.

As a young Dartmouth College graduate from Brooklyn, Paul Binder had tried various jobs. Dissatisfied with the direction of his life, he joined the San Francisco Mime Troupe. Besides performing and juggling, he learned to express emotions through physical means, as well as the importance of making audience contact. But at the time, he had no idea where all this might lead.

He made friends with a young actor named Michael Christensen. Together they took a two-year journey juggling their way through Europe. In Paris, they were invited to juggle for a newly formed one-ring circus called the Nouveau Cirque de Paris. The beauty and response that Paul discovered there would profoundly shape his life. "This is home," he thought. "This is what I want, but with an American flavor."

When he returned to New York, Paul brought the circus magic with him. His dream was to form the Big Apple Circus and The New York School for Circus Arts, which would provide talent for the circus. With the help of friends and enthusiasts, plans were drawn up. A board of directors was formed, with Alan Slifka as chairman. It was decided that the circus would be a nonprofit organization, thus freeing it from relying solely on ticket sales to cover expenses.

After long months of training performers, working out details, and enduring setbacks, Paul Binder's dream finally came to life. The baggy green tent opened its flaps to the public. New York finally had its own circus.

The Big Apple Circus had struck a responsive chord, for its fortunes grew rapidly. In its third year, it toured the five boroughs of New York; and the fourth year saw the circus performing in Damrosch Park at Lincoln Center, where it leaped into public view.

From the start, Paul Binder acted as manager and artistic director of the circus. He also clowned and juggled with Michael Christensen. Part of the time he acted as ringmaster, a role he quickly grew into. As artistic director, Paul is also creator of the show. With Michael and associate director Dominique Jando, he develops a new program each year.

With the New York performance at Lincoln Center, a larger and more regular audience came to the circus. The show could now attract top-quality performers. The 1983–1984 season included five acts that were winners of awards at the International Circus Festival of Monte-Carlo, the highest awards in the circus world. Gradually a bond grew between the company members, something Paul had been striving to create. With so many individual interests tending to go in their own directions, this was no easy task. Now that the seed had been planted, the unique character of the circus could blossom. A strong company devoted to the creation of great circus would ensure continuity from one year to the next and greatly contribute to its development. The Big Apple Circus was maturing.

Paul Binder is a tall, handsome man with the look of someone who knows he is doing something right. "All the performing arts came from tribal rituals from our earliest cultures," he explains. "The circus remains closest in form to this original theater. Like those rituals, we transform the audience, taking it to another dimension. We can see this happen in their faces. Even the performers are transformed. How do we do this? We create magic. We use natural forces to create extraordinary things. The ugliness of the everyday world is transformed. And by making what we do look easy, we show people that they can go on, survive, and conquer their difficulties.

"Our audience comes back year after year," Paul goes on, "so we try to educate them about the roots of the circus. One year our theme was 'La Belle Époque,' the golden age of the circus that we see in the paintings of Toulouse-Lautrec and Degas. Another year we had a tribute to the first circuses in America. Next came Carnivale, an exuberant expression of merrymaking."

A recent movement in Europe called the "New Circus" has strongly influenced the form of the Big Apple Circus. This traditional one-ring circus emphasizes theatricality rather than spectacle. It evokes a wide range of feelings with the use of strong lighting and music. The Big Apple Circus uses this form, but with a strong American flavor. Although the circus is international in character, the style, tempo, and sensibility are strongly American. The energy of the performance is similar to that of a Broadway show, and the use of international acts with company acts to express a theme is unique in American circus.

If the Big Apple Circus stays closely in touch with its roots, that is in great part due to the presence of Dominique Jando, who is a circus historian and Paul's co-creator. He has a rich background in circus. For ten years he was general secretary to the Cirque Gruss in Paris (a leader in New Circus) and head of its circus school. He is also head of The New York School for Circus Arts, which trains youngsters in conjunction with Harbor Junior High School for the Performing Arts, a New York City public school. "It's useful to know the past," Jando explains. "So many of the old acts were fantastic; we try to revive them. By elevating the circus to an art form, we are helping to revive it and make its survival possible. Being nonprofit allows us a certain amount of artistic freedom. Not being dependent on sales to cover costs, we can concentrate on artistry. Imagination costs," he goes on. "A circus is as expensive as an opera or ballet. Here each performer is a star!"

PREPARATIONS

During the season, a circus performer creates a work of art twice a day; then it's gone. Like his or her art, the life of a circus performer is transient and cyclical. At the Big Apple Circus, there are two performing seasons each year: the winter season runs from November to January, and the summer season from April to August. Between seasons, there is a period of quiet, a time to go "home." This is a special time to be with the family, work on new acts, and regroup one's energy for the new season. "I love going home," says Ricardo Gaona, a member of the trapeze act the Flying Gaonas. "But after a month or two, I start to get restless again." To some, home is in Florida. To others it is upstate New York.

As new acts begin to take shape and opening day approaches, the intensity of practice increases. Performers take a day off from practice to have their new costumes fitted. The fit must be perfect to withstand the strenuous wear costumes get. They are specially designed, sometimes using authentic patterns of the period that is the new season's theme.

A few days before rehearsal begins, a caravan of trailers carrying equipment and grounds personnel pulls up at the circus site. The tent arrives neatly folded on the back of a flatbed truck. During the course of the day, you can watch it spring to life like a giant mushroom after a rain.

Erecting the tent is a long, complex process involving a large number of workers. First, electricians haul miles of cable, unload dozens of lights, and attach them to the cupola (the dome at the top of the tent). The four center poles are lifted upright with a special electric winch. The cupola is then raised up to the center poles with ropes and pulleys. The quarter poles are put into place to hold up the roof. Next come the side poles to hold up the edge. Sidewalls form the sides of the tent. To keep out the elements, all the seams are laced up, starting at the bottom and working up. By sunset, the tent stands erect, gently blowing in the evening breeze.

The next day, as workers are setting up the bleachers inside the tent, a dump truck backs into the tent and deposits a huge mound of dirt in the ring. The ring crew spreads the dirt evenly with shovels and rakes to form the floor of the ring. They top it off with a layer of sawdust. The smell of sawdust and damp earth fills the air. The finished ring now seems to be waiting expectantly for the hands, feet, and hooves that will soon be running, jumping, and flying over it.

Outside, the trailers of performers, crew, and their families are parked in rows like a fleet of silver ships. The horses are fed in their portable stalls. The elephants, tethered under the trees, toss hay onto their backs. Dogs and cats explore new surroundings, while children find bales of hay to play on. Pieces of equipment are strewn on the ground. The atmosphere is charged with excitement as old friends are reunited. If you listen carefully, you will hear a variety of languages being spoken among the performers, who come from many different countries.

At the Big Apple Circus, rehearsal starts the next morning and will continue for a full week. This is a longer period of time than at any other circus, which indicates how complex it is to coordinate performers, equipment, crew, lights, music, and animals.

Behind a table near the ring sit Paul, the director; Jando, his assistant; and Jan Kroeze, the lighting director. Each act will have time to work out the details of its routine. It is a slow process, requiring frequent stops.

"Hold it!" Paul cries out as the revolving-ladder act is barely under way. "The light isn't right on Jimmy and Phil." Jan makes a quick call on his headset. Immediately an electrician scrambles up a rope ladder to the cupola, swings to the offending light, and makes the adjustment. In minutes the show resumes.

"Watch this part, Rik," Paul interrupts again, addressing Rik Albani, the musical director. "We've changed the cue here. Wait for Phil to go up. That's where the music changes." He gestures with his hands. "Let's take it from the beginning. All the curtain pulls were late."

In the clown act, the spotlights follow the clowns around the ring. "Let's have all three spots on Michael!" Paul calls out. "And widen the spot here; he shouldn't step out of the light. Fade out as he exits."

The ring crew rushes in to take down one apparatus and set up the next in a matter of seconds. If there isn't enough time for the change, Paul may ask the clowns to rework their skit.

Rehearsal ends late in the day. Everyone is tired, but before breaking up, Paul holds a meeting in the ring to discuss the day's progress.

Watching the rehearsals progress day after day, the importance of the lighting and music in creating moods becomes apparent. "A circus performance is an emotional journey," explains Paul. "Each act may have many changes in mood. The lights and music heighten each mood.

"Our lighting is some of the most elaborate in the world," he continues. "When Jan wants to create a mysterious mood, he uses blue lights. When the clowns blow bubbles, three spotlights of red, green, and purple create a dramatic light similar to the colors reflected in bubbles."

In addition to considering the look he wants to create when designing the lighting, Jan must also be very aware of the special needs of each artist. The performer must see what he or she is doing during the act. In the tight-wire act, for example, the wire must be clearly lit, yet the light cannot shine in the performer's face, for this could cause a bad accident.

Of his job as musical director, Rik Albani says, "When you get the feeling out, there's nothing better. We use all kinds of music — contemporary, New Orleans jazz, rock, swing, classical, and some original compositions. We're the only circus that does this. It just knocks people out. Most circuses still use marches and waltzes. The children tell us when a piece of music works. When we play a song that they know, they clap along, and it seems like the whole tent is singing with us. Then we know we have it right."

The Big Apple Circus Band consists of eight members, including Rik's wife, Linda Hudes, who plays the synthesizer and composes original music for the circus. When Paul needs a piece to express a feeling or paint a picture, he describes to Linda the images and moods involved. Then she isolates herself for weeks at a time, looking for just the right melody.

There are many people working behind the scenes as well. Karyn Christensen, the wardrobe mistress, gets the costumes ready for the show, making sure they fit well, are clean, and are on hand for each act. She also helps performers make quick changes. Rob Libbon (Mr. Rob), the production manager, is responsible for the equipment, the tent, moving from place to place, and the crew. Sometimes he even acts as ringmaster, which, he says, is the fun part of the job.

In addition, there is a vast network of support people who contribute to the smooth functioning of the show: administrators, marketing and promotional staff, ring crew, maintenance workers, house managers, cooks, grooms, ushers, and concessionaires.

On the last day of practice, there is a full dress rehearsal. Camera shutters click, and video cameras roll to catch the performers in action. The evening news carries film segments informing the public of coming attractions, and reviews will appear in the morning papers.

On opening day, large crowds of schoolchildren arrive for the first show, filling the tent with their youthful energy. The evening performances attract more adults.

A performance is an interaction between performers and audience. Audiences vary greatly from one show to the next. They may be hard to please, slow to react, or appreciative and wildly enthusiastic. Since a performance is spontaneous and unpredictable, each show has its own character. In the ring, a joke or stunt may turn out differently from what was expected. A good performer is able to work with the moment as it happens. If a spinning plate falls off a stick and crashes on the juggler's head, he exaggerates his real surprise, creating a comic moment. If an acrobat slips off the wire, she makes it part of the act. When an animal misses a cue, the band plays on until the act has been completed.

Most shows proceed without a problem. Sometimes, though, a performer will make a wrong step, lose his or her balance, or miss a trick. When this happens, the audience can appreciate the difficulty of the act and realizes that these artists are really human beings doing extraordinary things.

Although mistakes are usually minor, occasionally a serious accident does happen. In one season, a performer was hit by the revolving ladder while attempting to jump on it. A few weeks later, a trapeze artist was injured while dropping into the net. Both performers returned to the ring after a period of recovery. Performers are well aware of the risks they take every day in the ring, no matter how many times they have performed the act successfully. They constantly watch for unforeseen circumstances and for feelings of overconfidence that can cause something to go wrong.

Like the rest of us, performers sometimes get sick, but few ever miss a performance. "It's a professional ethic," says Chela Gaona. "We can't let those people down. They came to see us. So if we aren't feeling well, we go out there anyway. And the funny thing is, the minute you start putting on your tights, it's magic! You don't feel sick anymore. You go out there and do the show. Afterward, you go home and collapse on the bed!"

Once the show settles into a routine, circus people find ways to use their time between shows. Those who perform with animals spend a lot of their time caring for them. The performers may visit with one another in their trailers, or venture into the cities for dinner, shopping, sightseeing, or visiting friends. Some pursue hobbies such as photography, sewing, writing, or welding. Often parents will work on the acts, with their children watching and sometimes joining in. Circus children develop a feeling for acrobatics just by being around it.

The new season means the beginning of school for the children of the circus. The One Ring Schoolhouse, recently organized by Michael Christensen, provides a certified teacher for the academic subjects. The teacher travels with the circus and takes advantage of the museums and cultural activities offered by the many cities the circus visits. In addition, to maintain the circus traditions, weekly classes in the circus arts are offered and taught by the performers themselves.

THE CURTAIN OPENS

As the lights lower, a spotlight appears in the center of the ring. Into it bounds the ringmaster, dressed in his red jacket, high boots, and shiny top hat. His face beams with pride as he welcomes the audience to the show. The band strikes up an infectious rhythm, the lights brighten, and the red curtain opens.

Out come the acrobats, jumping, tumbling, somersaulting.

Now the lights lower as the spotlight finds Vanessa Thomas spinning one Hula-Hoop around her waist, then two, then three. As she dances with all three hoops spinning, a murmur of admiration comes from the audience. Her bubbly energy sets a quick pace for the show.

Two jugglers toss rings up in the air with rapid-fire rhythm. They weave and dance around one another, playing leapfrog while keeping a flow of objects gliding through the air. Barrett Felker and Jim Strinka of the Dynamotion Jugglers are guest artists with precise timing and a lighthearted style.

EQUESTRIAN ARTISTRY

The lights lower to near darkness. A blue mist flows gently into the ring, while the music creates a mysterious mood. A figure in black cape and white mask appears, catching a large white hoop that rolls silently in. A golden horse with black feathers nodding from its head enters and steps back and forth through the hoop. As the lights go up and the music quickens, it breaks into a gallop around the ring, jumping through hoops and exiting through a paper-covered hoop. The figure takes off her mask. It is Katja Schumann, the circus's resident equestrienne.

As she stands in the center of the ring with a long whip and a billowing skirt, four horses gallop around her in unison. They jump in rhythm in and out of four large baskets on the ground. When the music changes, they stop, turn toward her, and, at her signal, rear on their hind legs. As a finale, she mounts one of the horses and jumps repeatedly through a hoop held by two riders going in the opposite direction. She exits with a jump through a paper hoop.

It is small wonder that Katja shows exceptional ability in working with horses. She comes from five generations of horse trainers. Her father, Max Schumann, is a master horseman and former director of the renowned Circus Schumann in Copenhagen. "I had a pretty normal childhood," Katja says. "I went to school like other children, but before and after school I hung out at the stables a lot. I guess I got in the way a bit, but I had a good time." She first performed in the ring at the age of three, with a pony named Chester.

Katja won the prestigious Prix de la Dame du Cirque at Monte-Carlo in 1974. She also received the Gold Medal at the Circus World Championships in London in 1976.

Katja came to the Big Apple Circus as a guest artist in 1981. Two years later, she joined the company. She also became Paul Binder's wife and mother of their two children. Paul likes to take part in the equestrian acts and often directs the horses from the center of the ring when Katja is performing.

When not on the road, Katja and Paul live in their trailer on an old horse farm in upstate New York. Katja has one groom and hires another during the show to take care of her eight horses. "You can do a lot with a few horses," she explains. When she was growing up, her father kept about a hundred horses. "But these days, everything is so expensive—the grooms, the hay, transportation."

She trains for about three hours a day. As she goes through her routines, you marvel at her ability to direct the horses using only words and gestures. "You must know what you want from a horse and how to get it," she explains. "If you don't, you're a poor trainer." Katja can achieve almost anything she needs with five basic verbal commands. "Brave" (as in "bravo"), meaning "brave" and "good," is the word she uses most. With it she reassures her horses constantly. Horses are easily confused and frightened. The leather pouch at her side is filled with sweet grain for further reinforcement. The whip is basically a pointer that indicates to the horse how fast and where it should go. Body language is the invisible tool that reinforces the others. A physical-emotional language between horse and trainer forms a foundation for creating equestrian art.

DANCING ON A WIRE ★

Once again the lights are lowered. The music takes on a lighthearted mood. The masked figure of a Harlequin appears, twirling a plate on a stick. Now in comes Columbine, who tickles him with a feather, takes his plate and stick, and swings up onto the tight wire, knocking him over as she does. Then these two characters vie for the audience's attention by trying to outdo each other on the wire. Columbine dances across the wire, stands on one leg, goes into a split, and finally walks across on toe shoes. Harlequin shows off with his own fancy footwork, jumps, and scissors. He goes into a back and then a front somersault. The forward somersault is an extraordinary feat, performed by David Dimitri as Harlequin. Marie Pierre Benac, as Columbine, is the essence of feminine grace.

"The circus is magic," Marie Pierre says. "I want to give people a beautiful illusion. I have a great respect for the body, and I want to make it beautiful by exercising." Before she could accomplish this, Marie Pierre had a major obstacle to overcome: as a child she had asthma. To strengthen her body, her parents sent her to a gymnastics school in the French Pyrenees. In time, the asthma disappeared. At the age of twenty, she joined the circus school of the Cirque Gruss, and within ten days she was performing in the ring.

"Performing on the tight wire is so difficult," explains David Dimitri, "that tight-wire performers usually perform only that one discipline; it requires a lifetime of dedication to become truly comfortable with it. Each trick must be highly controlled. There is no moment of ease on the wire; the acrobat must work to keep his or her balance every moment, for the wire vibrates in an up-and-down as well as sideways direction. It is a very risky act, for a fall on a quarter inch of steel wire can cause severe injury."

At the age of seven, David was clowning with his father in the Circus Knie in Switzerland. His father is Dimitri, a renowned clown, actor, and theater director who has also appeared at the Big Apple Circus. "From my father, I learned the importance of respect for my work, of perfection, and of constant practice. He is very exacting." By the age of sixteen, David had caught Paul Binder's eye, and he soon joined the Big Apple Circus. David has a strong background in dance, which helped him to develop a beautiful style of movement. He likes to entertain, to make people react. "It's important to excel in something, to stand out."

Before going into a somersault, David takes time to concentrate his mind and center his body on the wire. "An Olympic coach told me to pause before and after each somersault," he explains, "so my inner ears could adjust. After a somersault, I have trouble seeing the wire because my inner ears are confused." As he goes down for the jump, he breathes in; on landing, he breathes out. As he takes to the air, he can feel whether he is rotating too fast or too slowly, too high or too low, and he has time to compensate. With a perfect takeoff, he makes a perfect landing. The backward flip on the wire is difficult, but not unusual. The forward flip is breathtaking. It is so difficult that only a few acrobats attempt it. The acrobat's body blocks the view of the wire as he or she comes around, leaving the performer only an instant to adjust before landing. But David has the rare gift that allows him to feel where he is in space.

Both Marie Pierre and David participate in many of the company acts. They take part in the horse acts and perform as dancers and carpet acrobats. They are perfectionists and constant workers. To keep their performance excellent, they take time out every day to practice on the wire, even between performances. "I can never perform too much," admits Marie Pierre. "I love it. Once, in Switzerland, we had only one week off all year, and it was just fine!"

IT'S A DOG! ★

In the next act, Johnny Martin introduces his trick dog Lady. In a charming French accent, he pleads with her to do some of her tricks. "Jump through the hoop, Lady." Lady just sits there. "Please, Lady, jump on the table." But Lady is too tired. Johnny jumps on the table himself to coax her. "Please, Lady, bark!" But unfortunately, Lady can do nothing. In fact, she seems to become more limp and drapes herself like an old rag on his arm as he tries to help her up. When she goes backstage to change her costume, a much smaller dog returns. "Is your costume too tight?" Johnny asks. No, this is another dog—Gladys. And she can do something. She sits up, and as a finale, Johnny appears to do a headstand on her. The crowd loves it!

★

CLOWN ALLEY

The ring is dark once more. Then a red, green, and purple spotlight outlines the figure of Mr. Stubs, a bearded clown in tattered hat and coat. He is blowing bubbles. As they fall into the audience, people reach up to catch them. The ringmaster comes over to tell Mr. Stubs he can't do that here. So the clown picks up his belongings, takes them to the other side of the ring, and starts to blow more bubbles. Again the ringmaster comes over, and the scene is repeated. The next time this happens, the ringmaster takes the bubble-making equipment and drops it into a garbage can. The audience boos and hisses. Mr. Stubs gingerly approaches the can, lifts the top—and out pour hundreds of bubbles! Mr. Stubs, his eyes wide with delight, plays a little tune by popping them one by one. Finally he takes off his hat and dances through them, ecstatic. Slowly, the bubbles stop coming, and the lights turn off. The audience is entranced.

In America, the clown developed into a silly character to be laughed at; in Europe, the clown developed a more complex character with intelligence and wit. The clowns at the Big Apple Circus follow in the European tradition. They show us a wide range of human responses; we can easily laugh at their vulnerabilities as well as our own.

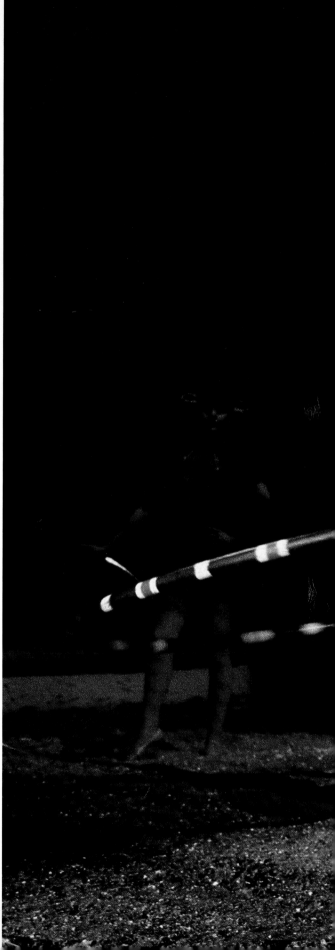

When Paul and Michael started clowning, Paul played an "Auguste" clown, while Michael played a white clown. Traditionally, the Auguste is frumpy, simple, and capable of outwitting the white clown by his innocence. The white clown, on the other hand, is elegant, sophisticated, witty, and quick on his feet. Michael Christensen felt uncomfortable in this character.

When Paul became ringmaster, Michael decided to become a hobo, America's contribution to clowning. He put on a pair of baggy pants and an old tux; he was whiskered and raggedy. That felt great! He was relaxed in the ring and having a wonderful time. He calls his character Mr. Stubs. Mr. Stubs can be naïve like a child, enthusiastic like a puppy, and even aggressive when excited. He can be silent and sad, but most of the time, he does all the talking.

For five years, the circus had an irresistible combination of clowns in Mr. Stubs, Gordoon, and Grandma. Gordoon is Jeff Gordon, and Grandma is Barry Lubin, who has since left the company. Over a period of time, the three became a dynamic and exciting ensemble. Their hilarious skits grew out of "noodle sessions," those times they got together to play with ideas and throw them around. "Bad ideas need to be pushed around a lot," explains Michael. "Good ideas just take off by themselves. Someone has an idea. We jump on it. It percolates. More ideas come. We work them out on our feet. Once there is a skeleton to work from, we try it out on the audience. We can see right away if it works. The idea changes as we work. When it has been tried fifty or sixty times, it is a mature piece. Yet the piece still changes. It is never finished. As soon as a piece comes together, it's gone; it's time to work out a new piece. That's the great frustration—digging up new material every year."

"When people respond, that's the greatest reward," says Barry Lubin. "But when they don't, it's very difficult. You have to be sensitive to the audience, and go with it. Each performance and audience is different. If a clown finds something isn't working, he tries something else."

Before the show began, Grandma would shuffle through the crowd, dressed in her red coat and carrying a carpetbag. She'd ask adults to share their popcorn, and ask children if they were eating their vegetables and listening to their parents. In the ring, she would do things most old people would never try: swing on a trapeze, enter a beauty contest, or play basketball.

Jeff Gordon is the most physical of the clowns. He does most of the jumps, flips, and falls. He refers to circus as "poetry in motion." As a former diving champion, he has found a way to combine his love of movement with art through clowning. His character, Gordoon, is a well-intentioned oaf and unpredictable fox who is always messing things up.

In one of Jeff's best-known skits, he enters the ring clutching an armful of toilet paper rolls. One roll drops to the floor. As he bends over to pick it up, another falls. This scene is repeated several times, until Gordoon, exasperated, throws a roll out into the audience. A moment later, a shower of toilet paper pelts him from every direction, knocking him to the ground. When he tries to pick the rolls up, he discovers a very large blower. As he holds a roll over the blower, the toilet paper gradually unrolls into a large moving cloud of paper over Gordoon's head. Delighted by his surprising creation, he turns off the blower. The mass of paper falls on top of him. He exits, dancing joyously, wrapped in a robe of flowing toilet paper.

"The great privilege of a clown is to transform an ordinary object into a magical one," explains Jeff. He developed his toilet paper skit after discovering the blower in a hardware store. "Making the ordinary extraordinary—that's what I love about clowning. Although there are days when you just don't feel like putting on that makeup, the rewards are tremendous. I love it so much, none of it seems difficult. I feel like what I do is good for the world. The world needs lots more circuses. New York should have at least a dozen!"

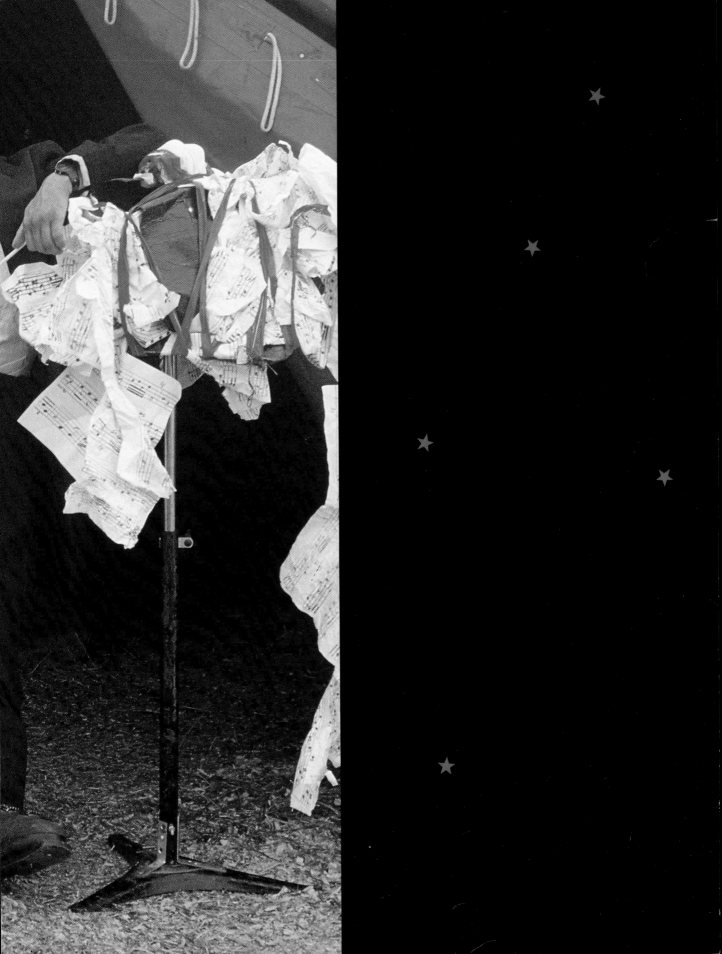

THE ROBOT CLOWN ★

"Mr. Paul! Mr. Paul, sir!" cries Mr. Stubs from the ring. He is carrying a plastic toy dashboard excitedly toward the ringmaster. "I've finally done it! I've invented the robot clown! Look. If you push here, he moves his arms. If you push there, he moves his legs. If you push this, he makes coffee!"

Into the ring waddles a clown with red hair, large buttons, and a windup key. He moves with a twitch and makes strange bleeping sounds. He tries to make friends in the audience, he squirts himself with a trick flower, and he gives himself a balloon heart, which flies away into the air. When he feels a little sad, he tickles himself with a feather. Happily, he discovers a trunk full of cream pies, all of which somehow end up in his own face. The children howl!

Denis Lacombe, the man behind the robot face, is a dynamic young comic who comes as a guest from the Cirque de Soleil in Montreal, Canada. His sketches are cartoons—zany, exaggerated, and slapstick; yet the humor is also subtle enough to please adults in the audience. He is inspired by Red Skelton, Jerry Lewis, Buster Keaton, and Charlie Chaplin. His comedy is highly physical; he never speaks. In his sketch "The Maestro," he seems to be a small man wrestling with great music and modern technology. Denis is a very flexible comic who participates in comic skits with Mr. Stubs and Gordoon, as well as in the company acts.

THE ROMAN RINGS

The light in the ring glows a warm, sunny yellow as sea gull and ocean sounds set an exotic mood. Mr. Stubs and Gordoon, dressed for the beach, settle in for some sunbathing. Mr. Stubs finds a conch and blows into it. At its deep mellow tone, the curtain opens and a dazzling woman appears. She is wrapped in brilliant sequins, jewels, and plumes.

The sparkling apparition is Dolly Jacobs, who sheds her robe and shimmies up a rope to the Roman rings overhead. She twists herself into pretzel-like positions, touching her toes to her forehead. She starts to swing joyously and stretches into a split. Back in a sitting position, she lets go with her hands and drops to her knees while swinging. In a breathtaking finale, she leaps from the rings, somersaults in the air, and catches herself on a Spanish web (a vertical rope).

Dolly is one of the great female aerialists of our time. She is a classic American performer: glamorous, flamboyant, and athletic. The daughter of the famous clown Lou Jacobs, she started training at the Sarasota Circus School. She was introduced to the rings by her godmother, Margie Geiger (of the renowned high-wire act the Flying Wallendas). She found that the rings gave her a freedom of movement that she didn't find on the trapeze. At the time, no woman was performing on the rings. They were considered strenuous and dangerous—a man's domain.

★ **49** ★

Dolly had heard about the somersault from the rings, which had been performed about forty years earlier by Frank Shepherd. No one had done it since, so she had to figure out how it could be done. It is her most dangerous moment. The lighting must be just right, and the angle and distance of the rings to the web must be perfect. Her act won Dolly the Prix de la Dame du Cirque at the International Circus Festival of Monte-Carlo in 1977.

Pleasing an audience with athletic artistry is very satisfying to Dolly. "I love to see the children's faces," she says. "Performing takes all my energy." But she does find some spare time to design and create most of her stunning costumes.

THE ACROBATS

"From Torino, Italy, ladies and gentlemen, please welcome the Ariz Brothers!" announces the ringmaster, stepping aside for four young men who burst into the ring. Two of the men clasp hands to form a basket from which they propel a third man into a somersault. He lands back in the basket, does four somersaults in a row with a twist, then lands on the shoulders of one of his brothers. Finally, in an extraordinary display of acrobatics, the brothers form a three-man-high totem, one jumping up from the ground, the other flipped from the hands of his brothers to the top.

The audience has just seen a rare display of pure acrobatics, which is almost a lost art. Using no apparatus but the hands to propel an acrobat into the air is extremely difficult. It requires training from a very young age, which still occurs in Italian circus families. Armando, Ricardo, Rudi, and Uber Macaggi are fourth-generation acrobats. Coming from a small country that is home to more than three hundred circuses, the Ariz Brothers' guest act gives audiences an extraordinary glimpse into traditional family circus acts.

PONDEROUS PACHYDERMS!

The appearance of elephants in the ring brings a prehistoric presence of great power and mystery. How is it that such a strange and enormous creature is capable of performing with such grace and precision? Throughout the history of American circus, the public has shown a fascination with this unusual animal. At the Big Apple Circus, trainer Bill Woodcock steps back to let his elephants take center stage. Whether they are shaving one another in a barbershop scene, playing tipsy after drinking champagne, or walking on their hind legs, you scarcely notice the elegant figure in a black suit and white beard quietly talking to his animals.

"Elephants are extremely intelligent," Bill explains. "They understand dozens of words. But that intelligence can work both ways," he cautions. "It can be a great asset, and it can become a problem, too. If an elephant has been overtrained or poorly trained, it may become hard to handle." Bill is recognized as one of the greatest elephant trainers in the world today, a skill he learned from his father, also a renowned elephant trainer.

Bill can train an elephant in the basics in about six weeks. It is first taught submission to the trainer by "stretching out," or laying the animal down by pulling on a rope attached to one leg and slung over its back. Once the trainer has established himself as the "leader," the elephant is trained to go forward, back up, lift a leg, stand on its hind legs, and pick up objects with its trunk. This is accomplished through the use of language, a stick, and by physically pushing the elephant.

"Every elephant is an individual," says Bill. "If a trainer is very lucky, he may find an animal with exceptional talent and intelligence." This is the case with Bill's well-known elephant Anna May. She is recognized among circus people as the most intelligent elephant in the circus world. She has a large repertoire of tricks that she performs, and she can do them with minimum prompting. As she stands on a platform on her hind legs, or carries a member of the Woodcock family in her mouth, or gives a ride to one of the family panthers, she elicits unabashed admiration from the audience. Bill's wife, Barbara, knows Anna May is a very special elephant; Anna May saved Barbara's life once. "She was holding me in her mouth," Barbara explains, "and as the platform we were performing on collapsed, she held me up to keep me from being crushed under her weight."

Barbara is a big-cat trainer. She owns four leopards. "The cats are like pets to our family," she says. "Their nature is a lot like that of Siamese cats; they are very demanding and independent. You train cats with instincts and feelings. With an elephant, you talk things over."

UP IN THE AIR

"Come with us now to Carnivale in Rio with Phil Beder and Jim Tinsman!" To the brassy rhythms of the band, two young men leap onto a rotating ladder suspended over the ring. They sway back and forth, looking like a couple of kids who have just discovered a wildly swinging tree limb. With mischievous energy, they start to lose their balance, but catch themselves just at the last moment. When the ladder is perfectly balanced, they both go into a handstand. After a bit more comedy, the ladder goes into a wild spin, eliciting screams of delight from the children in the audience.

Jimmy engages the audience with friendly banter as he performs his daring and playful antics. His style of presentation is typically American: he seems like the bold, brash kid-next-door. Phil is the anchor of the team. While Jimmy fools around, Phil counterbalances his every move, never taking his eyes off him. Phil loves working on the revolving ladder and has a healthy respect for heights. "For me," Jimmy says, "the higher the act is, the better. What's the sense of living if you can't feel your heart beat!"

Jim Tinsman designed the ladder. As a youngster, he never had any formal training in acrobatics. A promoter for Ringling Brothers saw him clowning at a party once and suggested he try Clown College. While there, he learned hand balancing. He got hooked on it. Since joining the Big Apple Circus, he has performed his own hand-balancing acts and participates in the company acts. Phil began as a gymnastics competitor in New York. He taught at The New York School for Circus Arts before joining the Cirque Gruss in Paris and now the Big Apple Circus.

Another wonderful aerial act is "A Flight by Tisha." Tisha Tinsman, Jimmy's wife, swings high above the ring on a double rope swing. Dressed in a white costume with delicate plumage, she resembles an exquisite bird as she balances at the waist, drops to one foot, and flips over repeatedly on the ropes. As a finale, she descends from the top of the tent, spinning from a neck loop.

Tisha came to the Big Apple Circus with a background in dance. Here she has performed an aerial butterfly act and is a regular in company acts. In the ring, she forms an easy contact with the audience. She is glamorous and playful and makes the audience feel as if she is one of them. In this way, her presentation is typically American. Of the Big Apple Circus, she says, "Everyone looks like they're having a good time in the ring. That doesn't happen anywhere else."

GREAT SPINNING TOPS! ★

"Ladies and gentlemen, from Japan, please welcome Koma Zuru!" Entering the ring, top-spinner
Koma Zuru tosses a large wooden top out at the
audience, jerks it back, and catches it spinning in
the palm of his hand. He balances it on a finger,
then in his mouth. He tosses a small spinning top
between two sticks while dancing around the ring.
He places a spinning top on the edge of a closed
fan, opens the fan, then closes it again without
disturbing the top. He puts a spinning top on the
edge of a sword, letting it make its way down
the edge until, with a quick move, he lifts it onto
the point of the sword. As a finale, a small top spins
its way up a string to a lantern, which opens,
spilling out strings of colored lights.

This is undoubtedly one of the most unusual guest acts in the circus. Top-spinning is an art that dates back to the fifteenth century, when it was performed for Japanese royalty. Koma Zuru is the seventh generation of top-spinners in his family, and the last one left in Japan.

THE FLYING TRAPEZE

To see the Flying Gaonas perform is to know the joy of flying. The most popular act at the Big Apple Circus is also one of the greatest flying acts of all time. It is the only flying act to win the Gold Clown Award at the International Circus Festival of Monte-Carlo.

The Gaonas are siblings. Armando, Chela, and Tito have been flying together for twenty-five years, longer than any other trapeze act. In 1979 they were joined by their younger brother, Ricardo. Their powerful act originates in the strong roots of this Mexican family. Their father, Victor, has been a circus performer since the age of three. He was their teacher and catcher and is still their adviser.

For the first ten years, the Gaonas performed a trampoline act. Then, one day, something changed their lives. While performing for the Clyde Beatty Circus, the whole family went to see the movie *Trapeze,* with Tony Curtis. From that moment, Tito knew he wanted to fly. They all did. Tito was fifteen then. Victor could see that his son was meant to fly. He predicted that Tito would be the best flier in the world and that he would bring back the triple somersault, which had not been done since 1932. He started to coach his children.

Victor was right. In 1964 Tito performed his first triple at the age of seventeen. The next year, the Gaonas flew for Ringling Brothers. Tito created many spectacular tricks. In practice he achieved the quadruple somersault (it had never been done before). He has already performed 12,700 triple somersaults.

Armando is the oldest of the group. He is the catcher. He was a flier for many years but doesn't really miss it. He sees flying from another perspective — upside down. "Of course, I am no longer the center of attention, but if I want attention, I only have to drop one of my brothers," he says jokingly. "Then everyone looks at me."

Being catcher is a difficult and responsible job. Armando worries for everybody. Since there is no preset order of tricks, he watches carefully for signals. Once the flier leaves the platform, Armando stays in constant visual contact with him. He has a fraction of a second to decide if a flier will be early, late, or just on time. If the flier breaks too early, Armando avoids crashing into him. Aerialists have been known to crash heads. Just before the curtain opens, Armando feels the weight of responsibility for his brothers and sister. But once they are in the ring, they have a good time. Up on the apparatus, they tell jokes, and the audience can see they are enjoying themselves.

"People always ask, 'Isn't flying dangerous?' Sure it's dangerous!" explains their sister, Chela. "But I knew a flier who killed himself walking down the stairs of his trailer! We love what we do; that is the most important thing!

"People also say, 'But you have a net to catch you,' " Chela goes on. "They don't realize how dangerous the net can be. You have to know how to fall; otherwise you can get badly hurt." Chela did get hurt. Her arm went through the net as she fell, seriously injuring her shoulder. She was told she would never fly again. But she decided she wasn't going to sit around forever, and she started exercising her arm. Little by little, she got it back into shape.

In a breathtaking trick called the passing leap, she swings to Armando, who catches her by the legs. As she swings upside down, Ricardo swings over, passing over the top of the bar, and the two switch places. Chela makes one more swing back, and Ricardo joins her on the bar. They come back to the platform together.

As a toddler, Ricardo played on a trampoline right next to the trapeze. When he saw his brothers and sister working out, he would hold his hands up to be taken up, too. At four years of age, he was able to climb the ladder and drop into the net. At five, he performed as the youngest flier, swinging once and dropping into the net. "The apparatus was like a big swing set," he says. Now his little son Alex holds his hands up to be taken up, too, and plays on the trampoline.

Tito and Ricardo take turns performing their repertoire of tricks. Besides the triple somersault, they perform several tricks that combine somersaulting with a twist. This is such a difficult maneuver that many fliers cannot do it. In the double-double (the most difficult trick Tito invented), a double somersault is combined with a double twist. Sometimes Tito performs the triple somersault blindfolded. "I usually do my most difficult tricks for my own satisfaction, since most audiences don't understand what I'm doing." For a surprising finale, one of the brothers drops into the net and bounces back up, landing on the catcher's swing. The crowd breaks into thunderous applause. What a perfect ending to an exciting performance!

The houselights now come up to the energized melodies of the band. Performers step forward for a final bow. With bubbles gently falling in the air, they look into the crowd and wave good-bye. Paul raises his top hat in salute. The audience responds with rhythmic applause. The show ends on a wonderful high.

As the crowd moves out, children clutch their big balloons. Ushers retrieve lost hats, coats, and baby bottles. The ring crew sweeps the red carpet. As the last stragglers make their way out of the now quiet tent, the equipment is adjusted and checked. The vendors close up their stalls. The ring stands silent once more. Everything is ready for the next show.

ON THE ROAD

The big tent will come down and be put up many times as the Big Apple Circus visits the boroughs and outskirts of New York City. With summer approaching, it will meander throughout the northeastern states, putting down stakes on the shore of Lake Champlain, in front of the Philadelphia Museum of Art, on a pier in Boston Harbor, and on a green at Dartmouth College. In fact, traveling plans are being expanded to include points in the Midwest. The Big Apple Circus visits the major cities as well as the many small ones. It continues the traditions of the traveling circuses of the past.

Circus people especially look forward to visiting the small country towns. "The small towns evoke the values of our art," Paul remarks. "Here, we are in touch with natural forces. Our animals can graze in the farmers' fields, and no one gets upset if our vehicles drive over the grass." In town, the performers may be recognized and greeted with admiration. In the tent, audiences react with unbounded enthusiasm.

Before the circus arrives in town, a local sponsor has prepared the community for its arrival. Museums and colleges help to promote the circus as an art form, and in return, they share proceeds from the ticket sales for their own organizations.

With the coming of the long, hot days of August, the performance season comes to an end. The big blue-and-white tent with the bright red stars is folded up, and the performers head for home and a brief rest. Soon a new cycle of training, rehearsal, and performance will begin again.

In the old days, when a circus pulled into town, it seemed like a messenger from another world. It had come from far-off places, bringing with it wonder and excitement and fantasy. Here, everything was possible. You could dream of riding galloping steeds, of dazzling with sequins and plumes, of testing your courage in the air.

Just when the circus in America seemed all but forgotten, the creative vision of one man has captured our imagination and is now redefining circus in America. Many have noted its success. Some are trying to imitate it.

Today the Big Apple Circus continues to bring us excitement, wonder, and joy. It stirs the heart and soul. It touches the past and reaches for the future. It is a testament to youth, inviting us to dream and to dare. The circus is international in scope. It speaks a universal language anyone can understand—young and old, rich and poor, civilized and primitive. In a chaotic world of technology and change, it finds simplicity and order. It connects us to ourselves, our dreams, our possibilities.

At the heart of the circus is a magic ring. Sitting around it we see one another's faces and those of the performers. We are drawn close together by the beauty, marvels, and mystery we find there. We join one another in joyful celebration. Such is the power of the Big Apple Circus!

★ 72 ★

50 3/06 (03)
50 3/05